What they say about
A Turn in the Grave...

"A blunderfully death-scriptive book."

Cyril Specter

"Put this book down immediately, you festering boil!"

Aunt Mildred

"Hah hah hah hah hah hah hah hah hah hah!"

Cuddles the hyena

"The worst book I've ever read. Arrant poppycock. I would like to steer you instead to my renowned classic, *Skipping to the Sewing-Machine Shop with my Aunt Betty*."

Cyril Clegg

"Bowvayne is the second-best writer in the entire history of the universe!" **Danny Cloke**

"Hee hee hee hee hee hee hee hee hee hee!"

Cuddles the hyena

"This book made me into a multi-millionaire. It could happen to you." **Mrs. Boatswain**

"Ho ho ho ho ho ho ho ho ho ho!" **Cuddles the hyena**

"This book should be banned!" **Miss Snodgrass**

B OWVAYNE has been writing ever since he could hold a pencil. In fact, it's hard to stop him! When he's not covering his house with notes, plans and diagrams for his next novel, he can be found writing screenplays, presenting television programs, or completing his first pop album.

Bowvayne first hit the headlines with his famous Mythbusting, which appeared both on television and in a series of best-selling books. He and his team of intrepid Mythbusters investigated mysteries all over the world, including monsters, UFOs, ghosts and buried treasure. This may have been what sparked his affinity with the spirit world, and enabled him to receive communications from Cyril Specter...

Born in England, Bowvayne now spends most of his time in Australia, where he can watch the sun set over the sea from his desk.

Visit his *fantabulous* website to find out more:
www.bowvayne.com

For more *Misadventures of Danny Cloke* read...

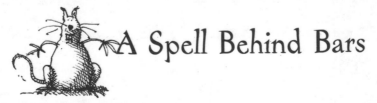 A Spell Behind Bars

The Misadventures of Danny Cloke

A Turn in the Grave

by
Bowvayne

With *splendiferous* pictures
by Alan Snow

USBORNE

To Eddie, John and Robyn Vermeer,
for helping Danny out of his coffin.
To Dad, for keeping Danny's feet on the ground.
And to Megan, Rebecca, and everyone at Usborne,
for making Danny fly.

First published in the UK in 2004 by Usborne Publishing Ltd,
Usborne House, 83-85 Saffron Hill, London EC1N 8RT, England.
www.usborne.com

A catalogue record for this title is available
from the British Library.

UK ISBN 0 7460 6027 0

First published in America in 2006. AE
American ISBN 0 7945 1292 5
FMAMJJASOND/06

Printed in India.

Contents

The following is based on the spooktacular story sent to Bowvayne by Cyril Specter.

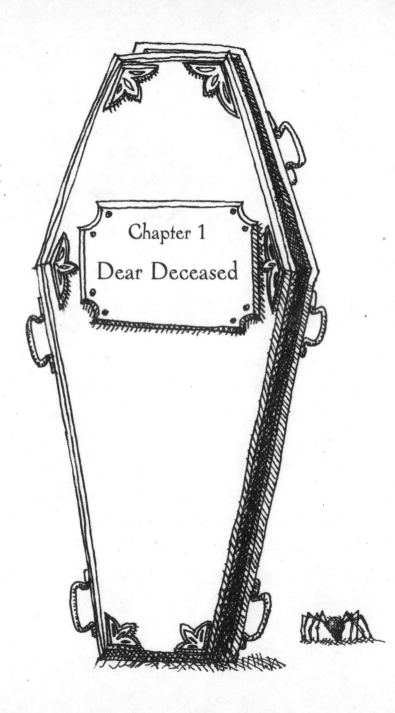

Chapter 1

Dear Deceased

ATTENTION: *Cyril Clegg*
Plot 9,345
Under-the-Sod Cemetery
Upon-the-Sod
Wessex
WX1 1SOD

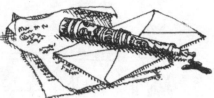

First day of Eternity

Dear Deceased,

The fact that you can read this letter means you are dead. I honestly hope you make a better job of death than you did of life. According to the S.A.I.N.T.s (governors of the Soul And Internal Naughtiness Tribunal), you were the most boring children's writer ever. There's more action and excitement to be found in a soggy cabbage leaf than in your stories.

Your books are used in some classrooms as a punishment tool. "If you don't stop talking, O'Reilly," one teacher said, "you'll have to read a chapter of Cyril Clegg's Skipping to the Sewing-Machine Shop with my Aunt Betty. *" You have caused children all over the world to get detentions for snoring*

8

in class. One unfortunate boy, a ten-year-old called Hank Pavlova, was caught talking in class, and forced to read the entire dreary contents of Plucking Chickens with my Mommy *fifty times*. The boy actually went crazy sometime during the thirty-first reading, and forever afterward believed he was a chicken.

It all ended tragically when he tried to pluck and prepare himself for a Sunday dinner.

Children want wonder and excitement and thrills and scares and magic and adventure and the occasional dirty word, not the steaming cowpies you deliver by the shovelful. The fact of the matter is that the only people who ever bought your books were members of S.L.A.Y. (the Society of Librarians Against Youth), a top-secret organization of child-haters dedicated to squashing the life spark and the joy out of youngsters. S.L.A.Y. deliberately turns them away from the path to Paradise, so that in adulthood they need to find some other, more sinister purpose to feel fulfilled in their lives.

Since that box of frozen fish sticks fell on your head at Al Cheepo's supermarket and ended your miserable life last week, the S.A.I.N.T.s have been in a meeting deciding on your fate. Here is our decision:

You are cursed to haunt Al Cheepo's supermarket until our Hero Hex is broken. The hex, or magic spell if you prefer, will stop you from climbing the stairs to Paradise until a child is so thrilled with one of your stories that he or she takes a turn in your grave to deliver you a fan letter.

Yours truly,

Saint Bernard,
Department of Boring Books

Cyril Clegg was sitting in an old chair in a waiting room that was somehow transparent and unreal. After finishing the letter, he stuffed it in his top pocket and groaned in despair.

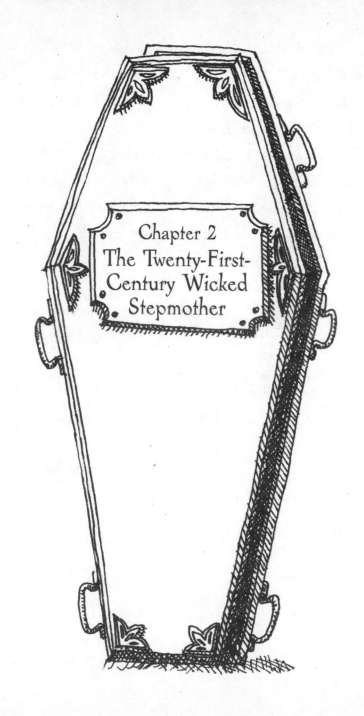

Chapter 2
The Twenty-First-
Century Wicked
Stepmother

"I'M OFF TO WORK NOW," Danny's father said to Danny on Saturday morning. "So try and help Mildred around the house."

· That was easier said than done, thought Danny. He always tried to help his stepmother as much as he could, but she had a way of twisting things to make him look foolish and get him into trouble when Dad got home from work.

"And don't go reading that strange stuff of yours, you know it only upsets her," his father added.

This was the worst thing he could have said. Immediately, Danny began thinking of the exciting book he was reading at the moment by the greatest writer in the entire history of the universe – Cyril Specter.

"Goodbye," Dad said cheerfully, then he was gone, the front door slamming behind him.

Danny's father always worked on Saturdays. It was the time Danny hated most in the whole week because there was no school and he was stuck in the same house as his real-life, twenty-first-century wicked stepmother.

The moment the door slammed shut, Danny knew Aunt Mildred would finish powdering her nose in front of the mirror in the master bedroom before preparing for her weekly Saturday sport – torturing him.

And sure enough, Danny heard her heavy, slippered feet make the loose boards creak as she came down the stairs. Halfway down, she caught sight of him before he had time to slink away.

Smiling her horrible lipless grimace, she said triumphantly, "Ah-ha! Your father says you're to help me today."

"And I will, Aunt Mildred."

He never called her "Mom" or "Mildred"; it always had to be "Aunt Mildred". It seemed illogical to him that he had to call his wicked stepmother "aunt". The first time she had ordered him to call her "*Aunt* Mildred", she stressed it as if she wished they weren't related at all.

Now she ordered, "I want you to clean out the hyena's house with soap and water."

Danny's heart sank. This was the worst chore ever devised. Aunt Mildred must have been the only person in the world with a pet laughing hyena. Its name was Cuddles and it lived in the garage. It refused to eat anything that wasn't rotten and stinky, which was the only reason it hadn't eaten Danny already. Cuddles had a fiendish laugh that chilled the blood, and if you were ever foolish enough to attempt to cuddle it, it would instantly try and bite your arm off with its powerful jaws.

Cuddles was a strange brute. Danny had learned

that it would never bite you if you looked it right in the eye. But if you forgot, Cuddles instantly latched its jaws on your ankle or backside. It was okay to throw it scraps to eat, but not to touch it. And you were certainly taking a terrible chance with your life if you went anywhere near where it slept. "Its corner" it was known as: a row of wooden boxes, stuffed with old papers, in the corner of the garage. If you ventured too near, the animal's fur would stand on end, its lips curl back to reveal dangerous teeth, and it would spring right for your throat. As Aunt Mildred had been the one to train it, presumably she'd taught Cuddles to do this. Three filthy rugs were draped across the top of the wooden boxes and this was where the hyena always slept.

But extraordinarily enough, when it was occasionally let into the house, it would seek out Aunt Mildred immediately and sit on her lap, and let her tickle its ears.

And now Danny had to go and clean out its smelly, rotten lair. His Saturday was ruined. Just as he knew it would be.

Danny did some quick equations. He was good at mental arithmetic:

- 4 sacks of rotten meat devoured per day = 16 "doings" per day.
- 16 "doings" per day x 7 days (when he'd last cleaned it out) equaled...

"It's the same every week. I have to scoop up a hundred and twelve 'doings'!"

Aunt Mildred heard the tone of displeasure (or was it disgust?) in Danny's voice. "You'd better not try and get out of *doing* it, you lazy little boy," she threatened him.

"But it's your hyena, Aunt Mildred."

"If there's any more whining from you, you'll spend the rest of the day locked in that garage," the wicked woman snapped.

Danny hurried off to get a shovel, some garbage bags, rags and a bucket of hot, soapy water. Wicked Aunt Mildred was relentless in setting him tasks like this. Danny could barely remember the blissful time before Aunt Mildred arrived, and he couldn't imagine a future that held out any promise beyond a lifetime of slave labor.

According to his father, Danny's mother had gone gallivanting off to Venezuela to hunt for the world's rarest bird, the Long-tailed Pink Polka-dotted Home-wrecking Cuckoo. They had never heard from her again.

When Aunt Mildred arrived on the scene, things went from bad to worse. Aunt Mildred was sly and clever, careful never to let her evil treatment of Danny be discovered by his dad. And Dad, the chairman of a widget factory, was staying away from the house for longer and longer these days. Danny thought it must be because Aunt Mildred was pressuring him to sell more widgets than ever before, or perhaps Dad wanted to keep clear of her as well. Although Danny loved him very much, he thought Dad was being totally unfair.

"All the other kids are out playing soccer or having adventures," he said to himself bitterly. "I think I'd just die of shame if I had to tell someone what I did on a Saturday. 'Oh, so you went to the new skateboard park, did you? I gave a hyena a laugh by cleaning up its *doings*.'"

"Aren't you out there yet?" roared Aunt Mildred, coming into the kitchen as Danny was filling a bucket with hot water.

"I'm almost ready!"

You just couldn't like Aunt Mildred, no matter how hard you tried and from whatever angle you looked at her.

She was beady-eyed and had a narrow, pinched nose and dyed blonde hair that was always fluffed up on top of her head like a pile of cotton candy. Danny couldn't believe his father found this large vulture of a woman beautiful in any way. He thought it much more likely that she had used black magic to bewitch him and keep him under her evil spell.

Danny knew that a lot of the other kids' stepmothers picked them up in their cars after school, and some even had strawberry milk and a jelly doughnut waiting on the front seat. Emma Chico's stepmother always made her her favorite foods: pancakes with maple syrup, southern-fried chicken, and corn on the cob. He knew because he was always trying to get invitations there. And he'd been told by another classmate, Mattie Deer, that his stepmother helped him with homework when he got stuck, and bought him books he wanted, not books he was made to read.

Aunt Mildred was not one of these stepmothers. At mealtimes, she would serve Danny's father a plate heaped with food, with the mashed potato shaped into a small hill. She would give herself a whole Mount Everest of potato. But if Danny's father wasn't around, Danny's plate would have such a pitiful amount that even a sparrow would gobble it up in one bite and still be hungry. If Dad was eating with them, Danny's portion would be adequate, but with hyena hair, or dirt, or even flies in it. Danny knew she was doing it on purpose, but the one time he had dared to mention it she became completely hysterical, crying and saying it was an accident. Then as soon as Dad wasn't around, Aunt Mildred forced him to clip Cuddles' toenails with a pair of garden shears. The hyena had bitten Danny and he needed seven stitches in the back of his hand

and injections for tetanus, rabies and hyenatitus. On reflection, eating dirt seemed the safer option.

Another of her favorite tricks was to go into his bedroom while he was at school and take his clothes out of the drawers and the wardrobe and throw them all over his bedroom floor. When Dad came home she would show him how untidy Danny had left his room and then he'd be in trouble.

Once she'd even written something rude in one of his homework notebooks, knowing the teacher would see it. Of course he was in big trouble with the old dragon Miss Snodgrass next day. When he'd tried to explain that it was his stepmother who had written "butt-trumpet", that only made matters worse. "Snotty" Snodgrass sent a note home saying Danny was telling terrible lies about Aunt Mildred.

To punish him, the wicked stepmother then piled all his toys in a heap in the garden and burned them.

Aunt Mildred's harsh voice pushed all these awful recollections to the back of his mind. "There's no soap in that bucket, you stupid boy."

Danny struggled outside carrying the bucket of

water, a garden shovel, a roll of garbage bags and a cake of soap. Aunt Mildred made him rip up his favorite pair of Cyril Specter Super-Pants to use as rags. He unfastened the special, reinforced catch, opened the side door to the garage and went in carefully, making sure Cuddles didn't get out. Aunt Mildred had threatened that if her darling hyena ever escaped, she would feed Danny to the lions at the zoo. He shuddered, securing the door firmly behind him. The only affection he'd ever seen Aunt Mildred display was toward the hyena. Even Dad was no more than a business arrangement to her. His business, Widgets for the Wealthy, had been in trouble and Aunt Mildred, a woman from a wealthy family, had helped him out.

The hyena laughed in Danny's face, and scuttled off into a corner. It's mocking me, Danny thought. It knows what I have to do and it's laughing at me.

Danny studied its bowl, crammed with rotten chicken and steak, the remains of last week's barbecue. As he took another step closer, the revolting smell was suddenly upon him, consuming him as completely as fog. The stink of the hyena, its rotten food and things far worse, wove their smelly spell into his clothes, his nose, his eyes and his hair.

As he bent down to start scraping, his eyes were stinging as if he had rubbed hot chili peppers into them. Scrape scrape scrape. He pried the first "doing" from the floor with his spade and its rancid waft made him retch.

"One hundred and eleven 'doings' to go," he spluttered. "One hundred and ten. One hundred and nine…"

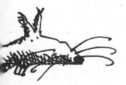

Chapter 3

Cyril Specter's
Books

DANNY WAS HIDING underneath his bed. It had taken him until two in the afternoon to finish doing the "doings" in the hyena's house. Exhausted, nauseous from the constant, foul odor, he'd immediately bolted to his room. He could hear Aunt Mildred stalking around the house, sticking her long nose into shadowy corners and dark places, hunting him like a cat stalking a mouse.

"Danny!" she screeched. "I know you can hear me, you festering boil! Danny, where are you hiding this time? You know I always find you in the end!" She took a special pleasure in discovering his latest hiding places, so that as the weeks dragged by, his safe sanctuaries from her had been eliminated one by one.

Figuring that she'd think hiding beneath the bed was too obvious a place to hide, Danny had actually outsmarted Aunt Mildred on this occasion, and gained some valuable extra minutes.

He couldn't understand why the world was so unfair; how she could get away with the terrible things she did without someone finding out and throwing her in jail. But what could he do? Tell someone? Dad didn't seem to listen these days. Since Mom had left, Dad had never been the same. Before Mom went she said he loved his work more than her; something like that.

Who else was there to turn to for help? The teachers? Police? A judge? But grown-ups always believed other grown-ups, not ten-year-old boys.

With a sigh he turned back to his hero Cyril Specter's latest book, *Mind the Step, Mother*. Danny liked the weird and wonderful words Cyril Specter used, like "heaving with gunge", "moving with mank", "hoppiting with

bities", "a ripe stinkulescence", "disgusterously slugable" and "smellisomely filthsome".

But most of all, Danny loved the stories. There were wicked stepmothers and stepfathers, horrible brothers and sisters, despicable aunts and uncles, crabby old teachers – all of them meeting a sticky, mucky end.

Wouldn't it be great to give Aunt Mildred a sticky, mucky end like the things that happened in a Cyril Specter story? He could send her into outer space to meet the terrifying brain-suckers from Pluto. Or her favorite restaurant, The Dragon Cave, could turn into a real dragon's cave and she could be cooked medium rare instead of her steak. Or he could buy a magic brew from three witches, pour it into her cup of coffee when she wasn't looking and transform her into a fat, warty toad.

He read some more from his book.

"I have just the vicious, *wishous*, delicious magic spell to solve your problem, young man," said Skeleton Jack. "All you have to do is believe magic is real and Uncle Vaughn will stop beating you. In fact, the most *spectaculous–*"

"Danny! If you haven't chopped the firewood by the time your father gets home, it's cockroaches in the soup for you!"

He heard her come into his bedroom. He hardly dared breathe. His heart pounded against the floorboards. Surely she'd hear it. He wondered, miserably, if his life would ever get any better than this.

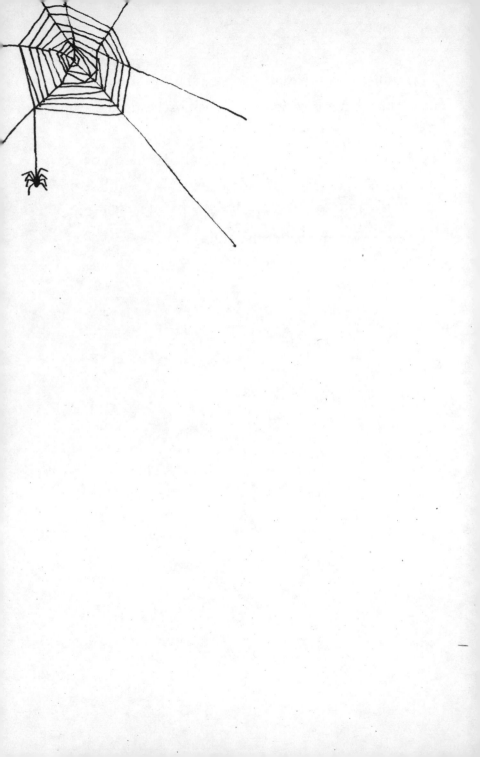

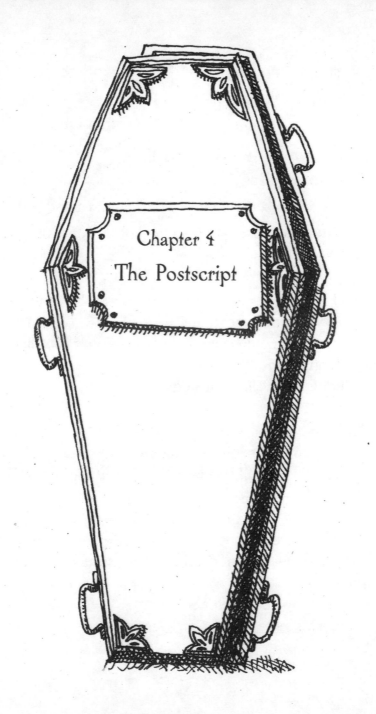

Chapter 4

The Postscript

A FTER A BRUSSELS SPROUT on a stale bread crust for dinner, Danny was sent to bed. His father still hadn't com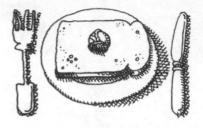

Leaving his bedroom door ajar, he used a chink of light from the landing to read the last few lines of his book.

...and so the evil Uncle Vaughn hid beneath the *rotstinky* compost heap, yelling that he was human – but no one could hear a word as he was slip-sliding about on his mouth!
That is, after all, what slugs do.

Danny sighed happily. He was about to put the book down when he remembered the message always written at the back of Cyril Specter's books. Turning to the last page, he found it there again.

P.S. Don't ever write to me unless you want to lose something dear to your heart, or you want a turn in the grave.
Under-the-Sod Publishers.
E-mail: <u>specterhaunts@alcheeposuper.com</u>

The warning was always the same. When Danny had read a Cyril Specter book for the first time, he thought the author would be just the man to write to for advice about Aunt Mildred...until he read those words about taking "a turn in the grave".

He'd heard kids at school talking about the *back page* of Cyril Specter books, and they always said the same thing; they'd never dare write to him. Anyone who knew as much as Cyril Specter did about making people meet sticky, mucky endings must be magical and spooky and terrible. Danny agreed. He'd never dared to write either. All the same, everyone thought it strange that part of the e-mail address was a particularly crummy local supermarket.

Danny lay awake, wondering how to get Cyril Specter's advice without writing to him. "A turn in the grave." What did that mean exactly? Danny didn't like the idea of being sent into outer space to die a horrible death at the hands (and hollow suction tongues) of the giant marsh mallowsquitoes from Pluto as in *The Space-Shuttle Vacuum Cleaner*. Or to be barbecued and eaten alive, which is what happened to Malicia Dreggs in *A Dragon of an Aunt Done Medium Rare*. Or to be transformed into an insect and die dramatically while hopping along a flea collar; a flea attempting to flee, like in *Horace: The Teacher's Pet Who Hopped with Bities*. Or slug repellent might finish me off, Danny thought nervously; remembering the tale he'd just finished. No, writing to Cyril Specter was definitely too risky.

He turned over. But could he sleep? Oh no. The wicked little thought nagged him and nagged him. How could he get Cyril Specter's advice without writing to him?

He glanced over at his favorite picture for inspiration: a hand-drawn pair of Long-tailed Pink Polka-dotted Home-wrecking Cuckoos. His mother had drawn them shortly before going away in search of these fabulous, rare birds. I have a few stories to tell her, Danny thought bleakly. If only I knew where she was.

Ah-ha, he thought suddenly. Hey presto! Eureka! I have the answer. I'll write down all the things Aunt Mildred does to me in the form of a story and just leave the ending blank. If Cyril Specter likes the story and fills in the ending, then I'll know what to do to Aunt Mildred! If he's angry because I've written, I'll say I wasn't writing to him, but sending an idea. Oh, magic! Oh, fantastic! My plan can't go wrong.

Looking at his clock, Danny saw that it was eleven-thirty. "If I hurry, I might finish by morning," he said to himself. "I'll creep into Dad's study and send an e-mail."

Danny felt his way carefully along the wall of the landing in the pitch blackness. Experience at avoiding Aunt Mildred had taught him to take one step and then a pause; in this way the sound of the notoriously squeaky floorboards was muffled. He fumbled about looking for the door handle to the study. Misjudging the distance he was from the door, his knuckles punched it sharply and, as it rattled, he gave a soft moan of pain and fear.

When he felt certain that Aunt Mildred wasn't about to descend upon him, screeching accusations, he turned the handle. Stepping inside he crept across the room, all the while running through in his mind the instructions his clever friend Tarquin Botfly had given him about working this particular type of computer and sending an e-mail from the address that Tarquin had set up for him.

There in the darkness of Dad's study, Danny sat typing his terrible tale, making sure to mention that Aunt Mildred had made him rip up his favorite pair of Cyril Specter Super-Pants.

When he'd finished, he clicked on the SEND button, his heart pounding. He wondered where in the world specterhaunts@alcheeposuper.com could possibly be.

Chapter 5
A Ghost on
the Screen

D ANNY WAS FIDGETY and nervous all day Sunday, as if there were hundreds of insects crawling and brawling inside his stomach. Had he done the right thing? "I don't think I'm very brave really," he said to himself as he dashed to the toilet for the thirteenth time that day. But nothing out of the ordinary happened all day, and as he fell asleep that night he felt strangely disappointed.

He didn't say a word about it to his friends in class on Monday, knowing they'd make him even more scared with their lurid tales of his approaching doom. But he was restless and couldn't concentrate and was told off by all his teachers, especially Snotty Snodgrass.

When the time came for his five-mile walk home, the insects buzzed around inside him dementedly; great fuzzy-bodied moths with wings that tickled as they treated his stomach like a midnight flame. But things were just as normal and as awful as ever once he arrived home. Aunt Mildred snarled at him for having dirty shoes. He had a soggy broccoli sandwich and then went to bed, before Dad came home again. That was something else she did on purpose; she made sure he and

Dad spent as little time together as possible.

Danny's last thought before falling asleep once more was that something bad happening to him might even be preferable to nothing happening at all.

He woke with a start.

A strange red glow in the shape of a perfect rectangle hovered before him. As Danny sat up, he realized that the eerie light was filtering through the gaps around his bedroom door. Although his heart was beating loudly, he knew he had to find out where it was coming from. Glancing at his clock, he saw it was exactly midnight.

He lay where he was for a moment longer. Could it be something to do with the letter he had written to Cyril Specter? His heart hammering even faster than before, he slipped quietly out of bed, put on his bathrobe and slippers and opened his door. He was immediately assailed by the red glow, stronger than before – as if he was wearing a pair of glasses with red lenses in them. Undeterred, he tiptoed along the landing, making sure he was absolutely silent. Whatever it was, good or bad, he at least wanted the opportunity to see it before it woke Aunt Mildred and any choice in the matter was denied him.

He entered the study. The light was almost blinding in its intensity. With a thrill of horror, he realized it was coming from the computer. Closer and closer he crept, a hand shielding his eyes.

As he got nearer the light faded, but Danny could make out the words A GHOST ON THE SCREEN flashing angrily, and then, quick as a whip, they were replaced by a picture of an ugly little creature that stared at him, as if ready to pounce.

Danny gasped and staggered backward. The creature was all teeth and claws and jagged edges; and entirely made up of letters of the alphabet that were the color of blood.

Then, to Danny's horror, the ghoul poured out of the computer like a red waterfall. With a scream he dived clear, and the inky red stuff that was once the ghoul stained into the rug right beside Danny's head. It sizzled angrily and plumes of bright red smoke rose up into the air.

As he lay there in despair, Danny thought it would have been better if the ghoul had killed him rather than ruin Aunt Mildred's expensive rug that had come all the way from Kashmir.

Wait a moment though, he thought, it's red writing. Reading by the light of the moon that came in through the big picture window, Danny read:

Dear Danny,

I do hate getting manuscripts sent to me and it is *loathly* that you do it. However, I steeled myself to read half of yours and I've got to be an *unliar* with you. It is a *stink grenade*. It does not seem to have any *munch* and *puscle* and no incentive to the child to long to turn over the page and see what's coming next. The language is *foggygetable* and there are virtually no laughs. You might say a giggler's graveyard.

I hated *criticrocodiling* your story but you did ask for it.

Further correspondence of any kind will see you losing something dear to your heart or having a turn in the grave.

Yours respecterly,

Cyril Specter

To Danny's relief, as soon as he had finished reading, the message simply faded away; the carpet was once again unblemished. About to sigh with relief, Danny suddenly heard the *flap flap* of Aunt Mildred's slippers as she advanced rapidly across the landing. "I'm sure I heard the little darling call out," he heard her say in the

saccharine tone that she always used when dealing with Danny when Dad was around.

Realizing he had only seconds to get himself back into his bed – and he couldn't exit through the study door because he would then be cut off from his room – he did the only thing open to him, literally.

He leaped across the room in two strides, bounded up onto the windowsill, swung out of the open window and across onto the drainpipe.

Perching there precariously, not daring to move, Danny considered what to do next. At least his bedroom window was open too. But how on earth was he going to get there?

There was only one option. Taking a deep breath, he leaped for his windowsill.

Fingers slipping on the polished, sloping stone, Danny scrambled breathlessly inside and sprinted for his bed.

Click! Danny's bedroom door opened and the light came on in a sudden blaze as Aunt Mildred stepped inside, a triumphant look on her face.

Danny lay beneath his covers with his eyes squeezed shut, attempting to make a sound like snoring, but trying to look angelic at the same time. Aunt Mildred's face crumpled in disappointment. She strode up to his bed and thrust her face so close to his that her hot, smelly breath almost overpowered him. "One second too late to catch you, wasn't I?" she hissed. "When you're really asleep, let your nightmares conjure up what will happen the next time you're out of bed and *you're* one second too late, and Cuddles is here waiting for a midnight snack!" She strode from the room.

The moment she left Danny felt total despair. Even his hero Cyril Specter hadn't provided an answer to his problem, and no end to the Aunt Mildred nightmare seemed to be in sight.

Chapter 6
Danny Sends
a Letter

N EXT MORNING Danny was throwing some leftover roast chicken and chicken bones from Aunt Mildred's dinner into Cuddles' bowl. (All Danny had been given for dinner was four pieces of alphabet pasta neatly laid out on his plate to spell B-R-A-T.) As the animal came scuttling toward him,

Danny said, "You stink!" Suddenly, he heard the soft step of a slippered foot behind him.

Aunt Mildred.

As he looked around, her eyes narrowed menacingly. "So that's your opinion of my priceless pet from the African savannah, is it? And *we* both know you were wandering about when you should have been in bed last night." Aunt Mildred gave him a last frosty stare before turning on her heel and going back inside.

All day at school Danny wondered how she would punish him for these misdemeanors. One thing was certain; there was no way he would get away with it. And when he got home he found out. The picture of the pair of Long-tailed Pink Polka-dotted Home-wrecking Cuckoos his mother had drawn for him lay on his bed, torn into such tiny pieces he didn't have a chance of putting it back together.

In its place was an enormous framed photograph of Aunt Mildred. It dominated the whole room, and her eyes seemed to follow him wherever he went.

Danny cried out in frustration and rage. "Argh! A turn in the grave has got to be better than this. I'd endure anything if only I could turn all of Aunt Mildred's badness back on herself."

"Danny," Aunt Mildred roared from downstairs, "stop talking to yourself and come and have your dinner!"

As he stumped down the stairs, Danny could hear the voice of her friend, Ruth Boatswain. He didn't understand how Aunt Mildred and Mrs. Boatswain could be friends. Although Ruth Boatswain managed one of the shops Aunt Mildred owned and didn't have as much money, his stepmother was still insanely jealous of her.

If Mrs. Boatswain got a new toaster, Aunt Mildred got a new kitchen. If Mrs. Boatswain went on a luxury cruise, Aunt Mildred bought a luxury boat.

The friendship brought out the worst aspects in Ruth Boatswain's personality as well, and it ended up with them both trying to score points against each other. Sitting in the same room as them and listening to their conversation was like being at a tennis match with its verbal volleys, lobs, smashes and cross-court winners. When they said "Goodbye" you expected an umpire to announce: "Game, set and match."

Danny sat down at the kitchen table in front of his dinner. Aunt Mildred and Ruth Boatswain were sitting comfortably in rocking chairs nearby, sipping red wine and watching him like snakes eyeing their prey.

"That lot will make you grow up big and strong," Mrs. Boatswain said to Danny, then did a mock sniff at the aroma of his dinner. "Look at all that barbecued chicken." She was skinny with a sharp, angular face – like a rat's.

Looking down at his plate, Danny suddenly froze. It smelled terrible, rotten. There was dirty yellow and blackish fur in it, and ribbons of spittle.

The meal was leftovers from the hyena's bowl! He could see that it had been licked and chewed and spat out by Cuddles. He just couldn't bring himself to take that first bite.

Great tears welled up in his eyes. There seemed to be no end to the nightmare. The tears began making tracks down his cheeks.

"Stop that at once and eat your dinner, you little beast!" screeched Aunt Mildred.

"I've had enough of this!" Danny raged suddenly. "Just for once could I have a decent dinner?"

With eyes like razor blades, Aunt Mildred said slowly, "You ungrateful brat."

"Danny! That's a dreadful thing to say," said Mrs. Boatswain, and in her excitement the rocking chair shot backward and she threw a full glass of wine into her own face. When she'd wiped the wine from her eyes, she studied his plate more closely and recoiled, giving Mildred an odd look.

Aunt Mildred staggered unsteadily to her feet, her hands outstretched like claws. "See what I have to put up with, Ruth?"

Danny fled the scene, ran upstairs and hid beneath the table in his dad's study. Aunt Mildred was close behind, but didn't find his hiding place. She closed the door and he heard her going back downstairs, apparently giving up on the latest deadly game of hide-and-seek.

With a sigh of relief, he left his hiding spot and sat in his dad's chair, facing the computer screen. "I'm going to fix you once and for all, Mildred," he muttered darkly. Hands trembling, he began typing an e-mail.

Dear Mr. Specter,

I hope you are well. Congratulations on your latest book. It is awesome. The kids at school say the same except they don't dare to write and tell you.

That story I sent you about the twenty-first-century wicked stepmother was true. It is my stepmother. I would like you to help me give Aunt Mildred exactly what she deserves. I'm prepared to accept my punishment for writing to you – just as long as she gets hers.

We could come to some arrangement about payment. I've got $30.45 hidden in an old sock and an Easter egg from last year that I've only had one bite of. If that isn't satisfactory, I'll do anything. I'm desperate.

Yours sincerely,

Danny Cloke

He pushed a button and the e-mail was sent.

Chapter 7

Cyril Specter

NOTHING HAPPENED that night. Thursday came and went. After raw bacon fat on toast, he'd gone to bed and fallen asleep, disappointed again.

But late that night a sudden chill in the air disturbed his sleep.

He pulled his bedcovers more tightly around himself.

Then there was a noise like a whispering wind around gravestones.

Danny was terrified. But he sat bolt upright to face the unknown horror.

His heart nearly stopped when he saw it.

Floating in midair in front of him was a gruesome sight. It was a ghostly figure as translucent as mist. His face wizened and wicked and hairy as an old billy goat's. He wore an old-fashioned three-piece suit and a fob watch, all as white and insubstantial as the rest of him. There was a large button pinned to his lapel that shone out like a beacon. It was glowing blood red and simply read: S.L.A.Y.

The nastiest, bloodiest, scariest horror movie wouldn't have given Danny a worse fright than the one he got at that moment. He thought he would be slain in his bed

and that would be the end of it.

"I am yours *respecterly* Cyril Specter," said the apparition, in a voice like the rush of wind down a tunnel.

"Don't hurt me. I d-didn't mean to cause trouble...I was...I was desperate." Danny's mind darted to the threats at the back of the writer's novels. How he wished he'd never penned the unfinished story, or written that letter.

"What is done is done. Action leads to consequence," Cyril Specter whispered hoarsely. Then he added gravely, "You have unleashed the wild magic of the Hero Hex, the spell placed upon me by Saint Bernard. Who knows the byroads and skyroads this adventure will take us on now?"

As the author spoke, Danny noticed a most extraordinary sight. Above Cyril Specter's head a spectral box of fish sticks kept crashing into the top of his skull, then repeating the action, over and over again, as if caught in a time-loop. This image flickered in and out of vision, like a scene from an old movie where the film has become grainy and decayed.

Noticing the direction of Danny's gaze, the author said gruffly, "It's how I died. You get used to it after a while." Cyril Specter floated up toward the ceiling.

Face taut with terror, Danny asked, "Is something horrible going to happen to me – like in your books?"

Smiling slyly, Cyril replied, "You offered me a bargain in your letter. I am here to give you the terms. If you fail me, something *grotifying* will happen to you."

"I don't understand any of this," Danny said in a voice he couldn't stop from shaking. "I mean who, or what, are you?"

"I believe I am the first author to carry on writing after death! *Death-scribing*, you might say, eh?" he said, chuckling. "Oh, don't look so confused, young man. Death is just another phase. When a caterpillar grows old and fat and is eventually entombed in its chrysalis, it probably thinks that's the end. But it still becomes a butterfly, doesn't it?

"Anyway, all you need to know is that when I was alive I was famous for being the writer of the most *sleepcrashing* children's stories ever. It's just thankful that the box of frozen fish sticks fell on my head when it did, or I could have poisoned the *germinations* of generations of children."

Cyril Specter looked ashamed of himself suddenly. "The truth is I was an evil little *creeptoad*. I was in fact a member of S.L.A.Y. (the Society of Librarians Against Youth), a secret organization of child-haters dedicated to squashing the dancing *elflets* out of youngsters and turning them into adults of the most *snoreful* kind. I couldn't help it," he added quickly. "I had a *dreaderble* childhood myself – a rotten uncle used to beat me mercilessly – and when I grew up, the mere sound of children's laughter left me with a *toothsome gnashing*. So I attempted some sort of *pathetiful* revenge. I wrote books with titles like *Staying Inside all Summer and Doing Extra Homework* and *Boiling Cabbage One Hundred and Eighty-Five Different Ways* and *Let's Polish our Shoes and Shout Hooray…*"

Danny sharply cut across Cyril's speech, yelling, "You're Cyril Clegg? I just can't believe it! The best writer in the world is the ghost of the worst writer ever – that's crazy! This whole school year has been a nightmare because of you. D'you know our teacher, Miss Snodgrass, doesn't let us read anything else but those Clegg books. I swear she's your – what I mean is, your alive part's – biggest fan."

"Don't be too hasty to judge," the author pleaded. "While my body lies beyond the grave, my specter is made to haunt the *boresome* supermarket where I died. The S.A.I.N.T.s, governors of the Soul And Internal Naughtiness Tribunal, and guards to the stairs to

Paradise, put a magic spell on me – the Hero Hex. I was barred from Paradise and *bandy-banished* to Al Cheepo's. I sulked and skulked there for a year until I finally came up with a solution…"

Danny interrupted. "Dad found a fish's head in some vanilla ice cream he bought at Al Cheepo's once. And another time he found that the hamburgers had been made with horse manure. He doesn't go there any more."

"All my work," Cyril Specter said proudly. "Al the owner deserves it. He's a *crick'ed crominal.*" Then the specter remembered what he'd been talking about before. "Anyway, in order to break the Hero Hex and climb the stairs to Paradise I decided to write the most *spectertaining* children's books I *passibly* could, giving sad children hope, and making the happy ones even happier. Of course it would undo some of the stink I'd done in life by writing those Clegg stories. And I've made up some *swizzling* new words too. But more importantly, the magic spell can only be broken if someone – the 'Hero' of the Hex – writes me a fan letter. And delivers it to me – personally."

Danny smiled. "All right, how about this? I'll write

you a fan letter and bring it to you to break that hex thing, but please, you've got to help me give Aunt Mildred what she deserves. Is it a deal?"

Cyril Specter nodded. "Deal."

"But what I don't understand," Danny said after a moment's pause, "is why you put all that stuff at the back of your books about losing something you love and taking a turn in the grave? If you didn't do that, you would have had thousands of letters."

In a voice that sounded oddly cunning, Cyril Specter said, "The hex has more chance of being broken if the child is absolutely desperate for help and will fulfil all its terms. Your Aunt Mildred will get the *horridifying* lesson she deserves, but unless you then fulfil your half of the bargain, you will lose the thing you love most."

Danny thought about the agreement. Why was Cyril making such a fuss about not fulfilling the bargain? It was easy. To personally deliver a piece of fan mail to the supermarket, or at worst, a graveyard, in exchange for Aunt Mildred being taught a lesson, was more than he could possibly have wished for. And even if he failed for some strange reason, what would he lose?

He wondered what he did love most. Then it came to him. *I love my Cyril Specter books. It would be a shame to lose them, but as I've read them already…*

"Let's get started," Danny said. "But what are you going to do to her?"

"I am beyond time," Cyril Specter explained cryptically. "You see, for the dead, time has no meaning."

As Danny stared at him blankly, Cyril Specter went on, "So what this means is that as well as certain minor hexes that I can perform, I can conjure things up from anywhere. In the time it took you to blink a second ago, I *skulkified* into your local bookstore and plucked something from your favorite aisle. Then I arrived back here again at the precise moment your eyes first opened after finishing the blink." Seeing Danny's disapproving look, he added, "Oh, don't get *jitterous*, it's from one year in your future. You can't steal something that doesn't exist yet, now can you?"

Cyril threw him a children's novel that he plucked from thin air. Danny watched all this with his mouth hanging open. The book slipped through his fingers and fell on the floor.

"*Magnifantabulous* things from the past," Cyril Specter continued, beginning to enjoy himself. In his hands was an extinct dodo. The big gray bird made a fearful squawking noise before disappearing again.

"Wow!" exclaimed Danny excitedly. "My favorite animal ever! But what has this got to do with Aunt Mildred?"

"Well," said Cyril Specter thoughtfully. "I can conjure up things from *anywhen* I please." Between his thumb and forefinger the ghost held up a tiny green disc. "Would you care to read a magazine from the twenty-fifth century?" he said with a twinkle in his eye.

As Danny reached out for it, it disappeared. "I must not show the future," said Cyril Specter. "It is forbidden. For if you know it, you can change it, and if you can change it, it's not the future, and if it's not the future, something else is, and it's not the future that it should be…and…and then we're all *confuddled.*"

"That magazine was smaller than my little fingernail," cried Danny in amazement. Then he clapped his hands over his mouth to silence himself. He realized that his voice had been getting louder and louder, and he didn't want to risk waking Aunt Mildred.

Cyril Specter was clearly relishing having an audience. "Don't worry about Aunt Mildred, Danny. She won't spoil the fun tonight. She's sleeping very soundly. I've seen to that. Anyway, watch me! This is something else I can do!" he said boisterously. Instantly, Danny's little fingernail grew at an alarming rate, twisting around and around like a corkscrew and stretching forward impossibly, until it reached across the length of the room.

"Stop it!" he screamed.

"Oh, all right then," Cyril Specter said, looking disappointed, and when Danny looked down at his little fingernail, it was back to normal.

"Hundreds of years' growth in an instant," he boasted. "I can reverse things too. Would you like to experience being the primitive worm that your ancestors were millions and millions of years ago?"

"No - no, thanks," Danny said, beginning to get frightened again. "I thought you were on my side."

"I am," he said casually, and pointed at the awful picture of Aunt Mildred on Danny's bedroom wall. The photographic paper it was made from curled up as if it had aged a hundred years in an instant, turned brown and ripped and filled with holes. Then it vanished in a puff of dust.

Danny whistled. "Wow! Terrific! Sensational! Why would you want to go to Paradise when you can do stuff like that, and haunt people, and write cool books for kids?"

"Because I've seen Paradise," Cyril Specter said wistfully. "Or at least glimpsed it briefly." With that the author disappeared in a puff of smoke, until all that remained was a disembodied voice.

"Right then, the fun begins tomorrow – Friday the thirteenth!"

Chapter 8
The Fun Begins

AT BREAKFAST TIME on Friday the thirteenth, Danny sat at the kitchen table, eating that wonderful hot toast where the butter has melted into satisfying little golden pools. This is better than boiled houseflies on dried bread crusts, he thought to himself.

For some reason, his father had decided to leave for work an hour later this morning and had made breakfast. Now he was sitting with his feet propped up on another chair, chatting with Danny.

When he remembered what had happened the night before, Danny realized there was already a little of the supernatural at work. But this blissful scene was shattered as Aunt Mildred stormed into the room with Cuddles the hyena trotting briskly beside her. She stopped dead in her tracks and goggled in disbelief at what she saw.

Giving Danny a look more dreadful than the snake-haired Medusa when she turned people to stone, Aunt Mildred said in a soft tone, full of underlying menace, "That's my best bread you've given him, Terry. Anyway, what are you still doing here at this time of the morning? Getting lazy in your old age?"

"Something's wrong with the alarm clock this morning. Doesn't seem to know the time," Mr. Cloke said absently, smiling at his son. "I am the boss. Hardly going to fire myself for being late, eh, Danny?"

Danny returned his smile, and took another bite of heavenly, hot, buttered toast.

Making sure her husband didn't see, Aunt Mildred gave Danny another icy stare, eyes flashing with pure hatred.

Danny shivered. This business with the clocks has only made matters worse, he thought. Cyril Specter will have to do better than this.

Stalking to the microwave oven, Aunt Mildred took a large serving plate containing the enormous, steaming pile of fried food that she always had for breakfast, then sat at the table opposite them. "Did you microwave it for thirty-seven seconds to reheat this?" she said to her husband moodily. He nodded.

"These are chickens' eggs!" she said, looking up accusingly. "You know I like goose eggs!"

"We've run out," Dad said apologetically, adding, "Busy day today, Mildred?"

"Oh, just flat out; a very tough day. I'm at the hairdresser's first thing and then I'll go into the shop. And it's my bridge night tonight." She stabbed her fork into a suddenly glowing mushroom. From a hole in its stalk the head of a large worm was poking out. It was dead, blackened and now almost cremated from the microwave. Without seeing the worm, Aunt Mildred raised the fork to her lips...

"Aunt Mildred!" Danny cried out to warn her.

Completely ignoring him, she bit into the mushroom.

"Honeybunch, may I say something?" simpered Dad.

"What is it?"

"Danny was trying to tell you that there's a worm in your mushroom."

She looked at the now half-eaten mushroom. She froze. It was as if time stood still.

Then she let out a scream that actually shook the windows in their frames. Cuddles, who had surreptitiously been licking some old fat from a piece of tinfoil in the bin at the other end of the kitchen, raced to her side loyally, cackling threateningly all the while.

Danny stifled a grin.

Dad tried to pacify the hysterical woman.

And ten minutes later, just as Aunt Mildred was calming down, Danny didn't help the situation when he said, "It's all right, Aunt Mildred. There's only half a worm in the mushroom now."

Chapter 9
Troublemaker

"I 'LL DROP YOU OFF at school this morning," Dad said, smiling. "So there's no need to hurry. Pour us both another cup of coffee."

Terry Cloke was a handsome man when he smiled, tall with brown hair and green eyes – but usually he wore a serious businessman's frown that masked any joy he might have had in life. And Danny was just like his dad in looks…and like his dad, he hadn't had much to smile about in the past.

While they were drinking coffee, Aunt Mildred marched through the kitchen, after changing her bathrobe and slippers for a fashionable and expensive dress (and having washed out her mouth thoroughly).

Aunt Mildred owned vineyards, restaurants, a jeweler's, a chain of private libraries, an exotic pet store – all given to her by her wealthy parents – but her favorite possession was a fashion boutique in the town.

She often went there to boss the staff around and act spitefully toward the children waiting in the shop, while their mothers were in the dressing rooms, trying on clothes. The manager, Ruth Boatswain, was often heard to complain, "Sales are always better when Mrs.

Cloke isn't around. She's got about as much charm as a puff-adder!"

Without a word, Aunt Mildred strode arrogantly out through the sliding door at the far end of their long kitchen, then along the patio and into her car.

As Danny and Mr. Cloke watched her go they gasped in disbelief.

"Expensive dress," said Mr. Cloke, as they both watched the car back out of the driveway and into the street.

"Yes," said Danny. "But I wish she wouldn't tuck it into her underwear like that!"

They both exploded with laughter, and they laughed and they laughed until tears rolled down their cheeks.

Fifteen minutes later, Danny was being driven to school in Dad's Mercedes Benz.

Oh, thank you for this wonderful morning so far, Cyril Specter, Danny thought.

They were surprised when, only a little time later, they overtook Aunt Mildred driving her Aston Martin sports car on the main road.

"She left a fair while before us," mused Mr. Cloke.

"And look, Dad," Danny cried in amazement. "She can't be going more than five miles an hour. Usually she's a fast and aggressive driver."

"She's a fast and aggressive everything," Mr. Cloke said, and suddenly looked thoughtful.

When Danny glanced across at her again, it appeared that Aunt Mildred - as well as the car - was caught in some weird, slow-motion effect. All her movements had the appearance of a one-thousand-year-old tortoise. Her face had grown a dark-red color, as she seemed to fight with the wheel of the car.

A moment later, Danny and his dad passed a police officer who was directing traffic around a car that had broken down in the middle of the road. It was a very old-fashioned automobile with raised seats, leather top and spoked wheels. A strange mist poured out from under its bonnet. Ahead they could see the flashing blue lights of police cars.

Suddenly, Aunt Mildred shot past them. Her car was like a crazy and dangerous beast. It accelerated to one hundred and fifty miles an hour...swerved and dodged the cars ahead with incredible skill...and she wasn't even touching the steering wheel!

Danny and Mr. Cloke watched her flash by in a blur, her arms moving so quickly that she looked like a human octopus.

The police officer began talking into his walkie-talkie.

The pair was doubly surprised when they overtook Aunt Mildred for a second time. The traffic had thinned out and the road ahead was clear, but she lurched along at no more than nine miles an hour. The way she looked up to check the driver's mirror – with her head doing a sort of slow-motion roll – made her look completely demented.

"The woman's become unhinged," Danny's father muttered angrily to himself.

Three police cars with blue lights flashing waited in a rest area. A police officer got out of a car, and spoke into his walkie-talkie, then signaled to Aunt Mildred to pull over.

But the car responded by shooting up the road like an arrow from a bow.

As she burned up the road, scraping Dad's beloved Mercedes as she went, Mr. Cloke clutched his forehead and wailed, "Leaping lemmings! What does she think she's doing?"

Danny only smiled knowingly.

The officer leaped back into his car and they all came after her like angry wasps, sirens blazing and tires squealing as they burned rubber.

Six miles up the road, after Aunt Mildred had

somehow managed to wrestle the car to the curb, she tried to explain to six very angry officers what had happened.

As she stepped out onto the roadside, the younger officers couldn't help snickering when they saw that the back of her dress was tucked into her underwear.

After finally catching up with Aunt Mildred and her police pursuers Mr. Cloke parked behind her Aston Martin, and he and Danny listened to the conversation.

Danny's father was worried.

Danny tried to look worried.

Studying her driver's license, an outraged young officer said, "You must have touched one hundred and fifty miles an hour, Mrs. Cloke."

"There was something wrong with the car, I swear it," pleaded Aunt Mildred.

"The only thing wrong with the car is its driver," said an old sergeant, his voice dripping with sarcasm.

"We were only in the area because of the most unfortunate breakdown of that antique car in a very dangerous position," the officer went on. "We still haven't found the owner. Might as well be a ghost.

And you've made a difficult situation into a dangerous one by driving so recklessly…"

"You don't understand," she interrupted. "I only speed when I see police officers or police cars!"

"Oh, so you're a troublemaker then!" shouted the old sergeant, even angrier than before.

"No, Sergeant, no! I know you'll find this hard to believe, but this morning every time my car saw the police it had an overwhelming desire to break the law."

"I think you'd better come down to the station," said Sergeant Plodder.

"Please believe me," Aunt Mildred begged.

"It's not me you have to convince," Plodder added grimly. "It's the local traffic court on Monday morning."

"Come along quietly now, Mrs. Cloke," said another young officer.

"But…but…my hair appointment…"

She looked up at her husband with a helpless expression on her face, then was led away between two police officers.

As Danny watched her slinking toward one of the police cars, trying not to be noticed by passers-by, he thought how defeated she looked for once. When he glanced briefly at his dad, and saw him thin-lipped with disapproval, Danny realized that Aunt Mildred's comeuppance was well and truly under way.

The last they saw of her was the back of her head as the police car drove away.

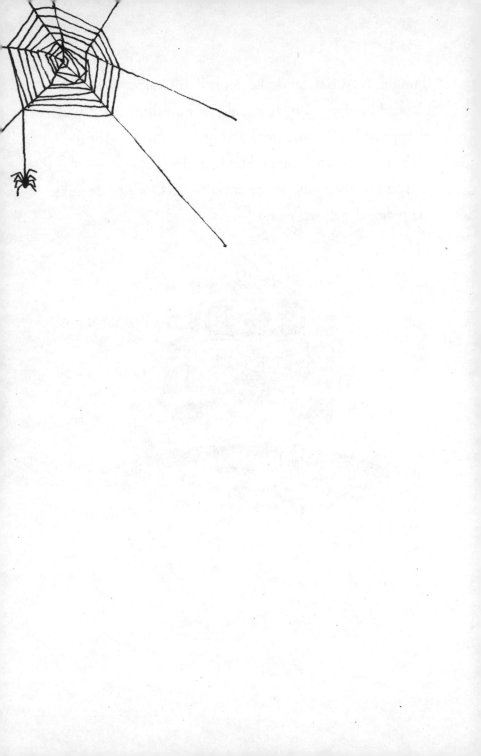

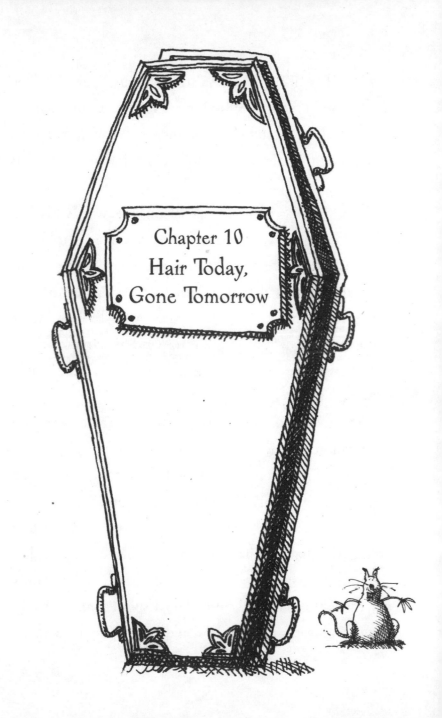

Chapter 10
Hair Today,
Gone Tomorrow

AUNT MILDRED WAS three hours late for her appointment at Strawberry's Hair & Beauty Salon.

She stalked in and gave the owner, Percy Strawberry, a look like thunder, daring him to say it was too late to see her.

If she had been a normal person, the weedy, lisping Mr. Strawberry would have flounced up and told her she was far too late and to make another appointment. But experience had taught him that saying no to Mrs. Cloke was like asking to have your arms broken. Apart from that, she was a good customer. She came in three times a week to have her ridiculous heap of cotton candy fussed over.

"Ah, good afternoon, Mrs. Cloke. You're a little late I see, but no matter. We can still take you."

"You'd better believe you'll still take me!" she shrieked, looking like some harpy of doom.

She was extremely particular about her hair. She told no one that her hair had gone an odd bluish-white color: not Ruth Boatswain, not even her husband, and certainly not that little pimple Danny. She'd spotted another two "blueys" this morning, so it would have to be dyed again.

"You're damaging your hair having it dyed so regularly, Mrs. Cloke," Percy Strawberry explained to her time and again.

But her reply was always the same. "Now listen, you pathetic wimp, you do the work and I pay for it. I don't come here for your advice."

She stamped down the aisle toward her usual spot, glad to have got through her dreadful morning. "I can just sit and relax for a while," she muttered to herself. "At least nothing can go wrong in here. I feel like losing my temper with Strawberry today, or at the very least, one of his dozy assistants. The awful cheekiness of some of those officers," she added sourly, still showing an awful amount of cheek herself where she hadn't yet untucked her dress from her underwear.

A teenage girl was walking toward Mildred Cloke, carrying two trays of hair cremes, mousses, conditioners and dyes. Suddenly, the girl slipped, and her legs pedaled furiously on the shiny floor, as if she were about to win a gold medal in an Olympic cycling event...and she blundered right into Aunt Mildred.

The tubes and tubs flew into the air, landed on the

polished floor and rolled in all directions.

"I…I…slipped," the girl stuttered, still dazed, and staring at the floor where there was no spillage or sticky patch to be seen.

"You brainless brat," snapped Aunt Mildred. "Still learning to walk, are you?" She sat down and loudly demanded a coffee.

Percy Strawberry raised his eyebrows heavenward and wondered what he'd done to deserve Mildred Cloke.

The teenage girl had a confused look on her face. Which products were for Mrs. Cloke and which for Mr. Strawberry's brother, Quentin?

One dye was called Hesta Medium and the other Extra-Strong Ratweed. One shampoo, Indigo Glow. A second, Wash & Wear. There were also unspecified tubs of Essence Of Scarab and Peach Bleach.

As he bustled down the salon, Mr. Strawberry cried, "No, Sue. The Hesta Medium. The Extra-Strong Ratweed isn't for Mrs. Cloke…"

"What!" roared Aunt Mildred. "I want the best there is. Do you mean to tell me you've been cheating me by only giving medium treatments instead of strong ones?

You scoundrel! I suppose you've done that so I have to come back more often and give you more money."

She prodded her finger into his bony chest. "I demand the extra-strong treatment."

"But you're damaging your hair by having it dyed so regularly…"

"Let's not go through all that again," Aunt Mildred said dangerously. "Just give me the full treatment."

With a shrug of resignation, Percy got to work on Mildred Cloke's hair. First he applied the Indigo Glow shampoo, then the Peach Bleach, and finally the Extra-Strong Ratweed.

Her hair felt tingly and alive. Positively glowing with health and vitality. "Don't rinse it, Strawberry," she ordered. "I'll do it myself when I get home."

"Mrs. Cloke, I really can't let you…"

"But I want the treatment to work right into the roots."

Still Percy protested. "It's totally against the rules…"

"Will an extra big tip stop your whining?"

Defeated, he wrapped her hair in a towel.

It was raining outside, so she put on her overcoat and

drew up the hood. She caught a taxi home, as it was too late to call in at the boutique.

Her car was still abandoned by the side of the road, but she'd leave it to Terry to arrange bringing it home.

When she got back to the house, she removed the towel from her head. After feeding Cuddles a pig's head, she checked the old wooden boxes in the garage to make sure her secret things were still safe. She gave a nod of satisfaction and then hurried inside.

She was about to get into the shower to rinse the dye out of her hair when a car horn sounded. Glancing out of the bedroom window, she saw that Terry had finished work early, so he had picked up Danny from school.

"What does he think he's doing, spending all his time with that carbuncle of a son. I've obviously been getting soft lately. We'll soon see about that."

Aunt Mildred's face was like someone eating crab apples when father and son came through the front door. She was about to lash them with her tongue when she saw they were looking at her oddly.

"What are you both goggling at?" she asked suspiciously.

Mr. Cloke could only let out a strangled gasp of horror.

Danny said finally, using one of his favorite Cyril Specter words, "Aunt Mildred, you look *hippoprepoceros!*"

She was worried now. It couldn't be that her dress was still tucked into her underwear; she'd fixed that half an hour ago. "What is it, Terry?"

"Your hair!" Danny's father spluttered finally. "You look like a French poodle gone wrong!"

"Or one of those fluorescent lights at the disco," Danny added, enjoying the fear that was on Aunt Mildred's face.

Aunt Mildred rushed to the mirror in the hallway. She stared in horror at the wildly tangled curls of fluorescent purple that cascaded from her head.

She put her hand up to touch it and a great tuft came away. "Argh!" she screamed. "What shall I do?"

"You could hire out your head and stand at the top of a lighthouse," said Danny. "You'd save them a fortune in electricity!"

Aunt Mildred could take no more. She dashed upstairs to rinse the dye out as quickly as possible.

But the sudden rush of air through her glowing locks was too much. By the time she reached the top of the stairs, her head was as bald as a baby's bottom.

 That night, just before Terry Cloke turned off their bedroom light, he looked at his sleeping wife, and her hairless, shriveled-looking head reminded him of a crocodile's egg.

Next day, Aunt Mildred bought a big, curly, bouffant wig the color of horse manure. From that moment on, every time next door's poodle, Pepe, spotted her, he howled plaintively as she passed by. He was deeply in dog-love.

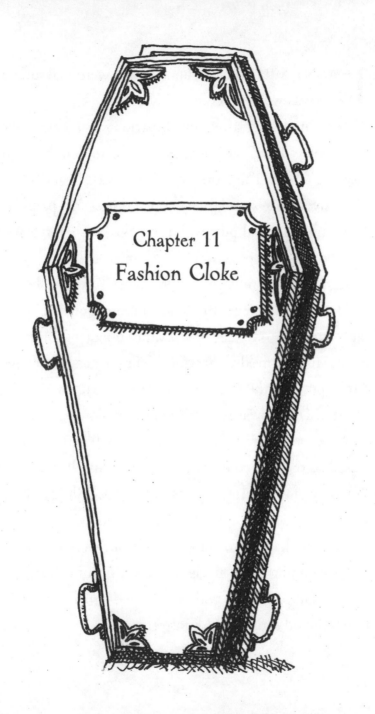

Chapter 11
Fashion Cloke

IF AUNT MILDRED thought things were bad already, there was worse to come.

Next morning, after an embarrassing incident with the poodle Pepe, she decided to go to her boutique, Fashion Cloke. The store was filled with beautiful and expensive dresses and jackets and skirts and pants and shoes and hats and purses (but no cloaks!). All the walls and the ceiling were covered with mirrors.

Ruth Boatswain groaned to herself when she saw Mildred coming into the store, before doing a double take when she saw her wig. Danny obediently followed Aunt Mildred inside, carrying a pile of heavy packages. After putting them on the counter next to the cash register, Danny was sent to the broom closet.

As Aunt Mildred slammed the door behind him, she hissed so only he could hear, "Think yourself lucky, boy. I'm only staying until lunchtime today." She'd brought Danny to the store, so father and son wouldn't be together if Terry did happen to come home from work early.

"Is he going to be all right in there?" Ruth Boatswain asked Aunt Mildred with a worried frown, as if she remembered something distasteful.

Aunt Mildred gave her a dismissive wave. "Oh, sure. He's a strange boy. He'll actually enjoy it."

"Mildred, that wig. It's slightly...er. Kind of..."

"What?" snapped Aunt Mildred.

"Um – poodle-like..."

Inside the broom closet, it was so dark that Danny couldn't see his hands in front of his face. Soon, he was bored to tears. And if he dared to come out before lunch, even for the toilet, Aunt Mildred had threatened to make him clean Cuddles' teeth with a wire brush.

Outside, Aunt Mildred stormed about like a tyrannosaurus with a toothache. She loved bossing everyone around, and she had a lot to take out on them today.

Danny pushed the broom closet's door open a fraction and peeped out. He could see everything that was going on reflected in all the mirrors. Suddenly, he noticed something odd about one of them. It looked all wobbly and misty. As Danny stared, the mist swirled and there, in the mirror, was Cyril Specter. He waved cheerfully.

"Mr. Specter!" Danny whispered in relief.

"How have you enjoyed the *spectabulous* show so far?" said Cyril, grinning impudently.

"*Enchanterous!*" said Danny, getting into the swing of Cyril-speak. "*Gigglarious!*"

"You're going to love the next part even more," said Cyril. "You do remember our pact, don't you?"

"Of course," Danny said, not really wanting to think about that right now.

"Well, just sit back and enjoy yourself." Cyril Specter vanished before Danny's eyes.

Blinking at the suddenness of Cyril's departure, Danny then glanced back out into the store. Aunt Mildred's loathsome figure filled a mirror.

He watched as she scowled at her reflection. "The wretched thing is making me look bigger around the hips than I really am."

Danny also saw that she looked about a hundred years old, just for an instant. Cyril Specter was at work again, he realized gleefully.

A customer entered the store.

"Morning, Lady Ponsonby," shouted Aunt Mildred.

"May I take your overcoat?" simpered Mrs. Boatswain.

"I've come here to buy something from you, not give away something," snapped the harebrained old crone, completely misunderstanding.

Lady Ponsonby was a tall and shriveled sourpuss of about seventy, terribly vain and with absolutely no reason; she had a body like gnarled driftwood and a face that looked as though she permanently chewed wasps. "I'm having a dinner party tonight and want to look incredible."

Cyril's disembodied voice floated around faintly. "You're off to a good start, Lady Ponsonby. You look inedible already." Danny laughed as quietly as he could, putting his hand over his mouth so he wouldn't be heard outside.

"What do you think of this one?" said Aunt Mildred, offering the old woman a gorgeous, shimmering red dress.

"Yes, all right," said Lady Ponsonby, disappearing into the dressing room, and Danny's entertainment was halted for a moment.

Then Lady Ponsonby stepped out of the cubicle grandly, did a little pirouette in the dress, and with a smile stepped right up in front of the mirror.

The smile faltered.

The poor woman in the reflection looked perfectly absurd. Her head was the size of a pinhead. Her arms and legs like matchsticks. In comparison the dress was like a tent for fifty soldiers.

The mirror was warping her like a magic mirror at a carnival.

The three women leaped backward when they saw the reflection.

In the broom closet, Danny was laughing uncontrollably.

The scream of fright and rage from Lady Ponsonby startled everyone. "I look like a circus tent!" she roared at Aunt Mildred. "Are you trying to make a monkey of me, you monstrous baggage?" With that, the old woman changed back into her original clothes and stormed out of the store, vowing never to return.

Aunt Mildred and Ruth Boatswain looked at one another in bemusement. "What did we do wrong?" they said at the same time.

The mirrors looked as flat as they always did, but had reflected strange, inexplicable things.

Mrs. Boatswain rubbed her eyes and forehead and said in an uncertain voice, "I...I...think we'd better...have a...have a coffee, Mildred."

"Good idea." Aunt Mildred looked at her own reflection again. Her hips were like a hippopotamus's.

Soon afterward, another lady came into the store. "Morning, Mrs. Bogan-Swithens," said Mrs. Boatswain.

"I'm looking for a hat to give me a sophisticated appearance for the races. I'm going to the dogs, actually," the woman said.

"You can say that again," Cyril Specter's voice whispered once more from somewhere within the closet so that only Danny could hear it.

Aunt Mildred suggested a green felt hat with a brim.

Mrs. Bogan-Swithens put it on and looked in the mirror.

The reflections of Aunt Mildred and Ruth Boatswain looked almost normal, Danny noticed. But Mrs. Bogan-Swithens was an extraordinary sight. Repulsive.

Her head was like a lumpy old potato. Her nose was hideously distorted and it curved in a graceless arc down to her waist. The hat was a pathetic green pea on that head.

Mrs. Bogan-Swithens calmly took a step back from the mirror and tore into Aunt Mildred with her purse, leaving the store only after a direct hit dislodged the hapless Mildred's wig.

Half an hour later, the store had lost its five most valuable customers.

Aunt Mildred was as white as a ghost and her hands were trembling. "What have I done to deserve this?" she wailed. "I can take no more!" she shrieked and called to Danny who had watched it all, "Come on, scab, we're going home."

Danny came out of the broom closet, grinning from ear to ear at the mirror's reflection of Aunt Mildred. She had two heads for kneecaps and her bottom was on her head.

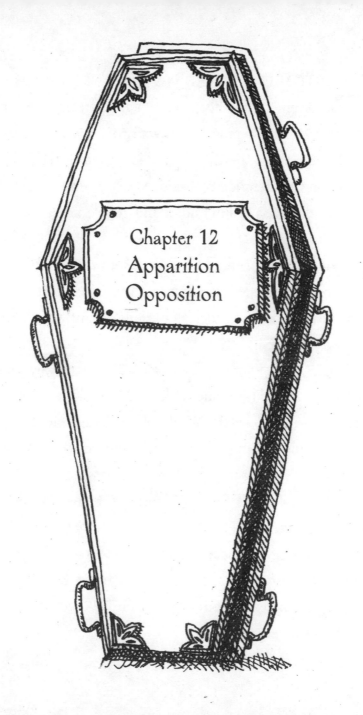

Chapter 12
Apparition
Opposition

AUNT MILDRED HAD just presented Danny with a rotten egg for his lunch when the telephone rang. As the wicked stepmother moved to answer it, Danny took advantage of the distraction to toss the odious snack in the direction of Cuddles. The hyena caught the egg while it was still in midair and gobbled it down, shell and all.

"Hello," Aunt Mildred bellowed into the receiver.

On the other end, a panicky Ruth Boatswain started gabbling without so much as a "Hello". Danny could hear every word clearly.

"That pizza joint opposite isn't a pizza joint any more. It's a fashion boutique called Apparitions' Apparel. They've ripped out the whole place, redecorated it, put up signs, moved in the stock and hundreds of people are in there. It's going to kill off our business…"

"*My* business," Aunt Mildred corrected her, then added suspiciously, "Have you been at the sherry, Boatswain?" It's impossible, she mused. How could a rival boutique spring up that quickly? They'd been selling pizzas less than two hours ago. Extensive renovations like that took weeks of work.

"No, I swear I haven't been drinking," pleaded a befuddled Mrs. Boatswain. "Just after you left, a whole army of men marched into Eatza Pizza. I say men, but there was something spooky about them all. They wore the sort of suits people get buried in, and they cast no shadows, and I swear I could see right through one of them and..."

"Pull yourself together, Boatswain. You're beginning to sound hysterical!"

"...and they ripped out all the ovens and everything, redecorated the place, painted the signs, wheeled in the stock..."

"You've already told me that," Aunt Mildred interrupted sharply, wondering if the woman had taken ill suddenly.

"...and they didn't even stop for coffee and cake every fifteen minutes like decorators normally do..."

Aunt Mildred didn't know how much more lunacy she could take. "You said hundreds of people were in there. How did they all hear about it then?" she said slowly.

"Ah, that's the worst part."

"The worst part! You mean it gets worse?" Her face

had gone the sickly green color of rotting fish.

"They've got a sign that says, 'Bring in the old, take out the new'! News like that travels fast. If you take your old clothes in there, they'll swap them for new ones! I've seen people walking in without a stitch of clothing on, wheeling in bulging suitcases! Some of those new clothes are worth hundreds of pounds! Even nicer than ours...yours, I mean.

"They're putting us out of business, Mildred," she went on. "Out of business, I say, Mildred. Hello? Hello, Mildred?"

But Mildred Cloke heard no more. She was stretched out on the carpet like a felled baobab tree. She had fainted.

Chapter 13

Lotto Fun

AUNT MILDRED FELT too unwell to leave her bed for the rest of Saturday.

Danny's dad had come home soon after she fainted. He insisted she go to bed while he fixed her a glass of his best brandy.

Initially pleased at this display of affection from her husband, her mood soon turned to rage when she heard him playing soccer in the garden with Danny a few minutes later. Terry had sent her to bed just to get rid of her! "I'll flay that boy alive!" she roared, and tried to get out of bed.

She felt weak and woozy. That brandy had been ever such a large one. Her eyelids felt as if they had lead weights tied to them...

Once she was asleep, Danny and his dad went to the zoo and then the movies.

The house was dark and empty when Aunt Mildred awoke. When she realized she'd actually been left alone, she was in a murderous temper. This hadn't happened in all the time the three of them had been together. She simply hadn't allowed it. "It'll be my turn to send them to bed next," she hissed. "Hospital beds!"

Moodily, she switched on the television.

"Saturday is Lucky Lotto night," squawked the television announcer. "And tonight some lucky person has just won seventy-two million dollars!"

A moment later the telephone on Aunt Mildred's bedside table rang.

Aunt Mildred answered it. For the first few moments she only heard a half-crazed woman screaming and shouting and jabbering. She thought it was a crank caller and was about to put the phone down, when Ruth Boatswain calmed down enough to say, "Well, talk to me, Mildred. Say something."

"What the blazes do you think you're doing shrieking at me like that? I haven't understood one word you've said."

"I said I've just won seventy-two million dollars in the Lucky Lotto!"

Aunt Mildred felt her heart sink into the pit of her stomach like a stone dropped into a deep lake. Only yesterday, Ruth Boatswain had said that she and her husband were going on a holiday to the Caribbean, so Aunt Mildred had decided to buy an apartment there. How could she compete with seventy-two million dollars?

"But the strangest thing," Ruth Boatswain went on thoughtfully, "was that I was on a train yesterday, and sitting opposite was a strange little man who looked like a goat; introduced himself as Cyril somebody-or-other. He was reading a newspaper, and when he'd finished with it, he gave it to me and just vanished.

"Anyway, when I woke up this morning, I heard on the radio all the news that I'd read in the paper yesterday...and although Roger wouldn't believe me, I realized I'd been reading today's paper *yesterday*! Couldn't prove it, of course, because I'd left the paper on the train. But I got sick of my beloved husband having a laugh at my expense, so I tried to remember the Lotto numbers. And hey presto!"

"Hey presto," Aunt Mildred repeated dully.

"Hey presto, my life's changed," Ruth Boatswain said, with sudden sincerity. "Being around you wasn't good for me. Like my heart was in the clutch of evil and greed. The moment I won, I saw what I'd become and am going to apologize to Roger. Promise that he can have every penny of the money if he wishes. He doesn't know yet. I'm going to surprise him in a moment. I'm quitting the store. I'm going to make something of my life. And try and help others too. Goodbye forever, Mildred," Ruth Boatswain said triumphantly and hung up the phone.

Ruth Boatswain's husband, Roger, had gone to the movies with Danny and his dad, and when it was over, Mr. Cloke had driven him home again. While the men had a quick game of pool and a beer, Danny went to get himself a Coke from the kitchen, all the while wondering how on earth Cyril Specter had managed to conjure the lotto numbers into Saturday's paper.

Pausing outside the door, he heard every word Mrs. Boatswain said to Aunt Mildred. For the first time, it occurred to Danny how mightily powerful Cyril Specter was – able to completely change the course of people's lives at a single whim – and he thought, with a twinge of fear, that he had better do nothing to upset him.

Chapter 14

Dirty Washing

AUNT MILDRED WOULD gladly let Ruth Boatswain win the Lotto again, or have another boutique spring up and put her out of business. Or have another crazy mirror drive away all her customers. She would gladly lose her hair again, have the car make a monkey of her, get arrested. She would swallow a whole worm if she could have stopped what was to follow.

It all started with the clothes in her closet throwing

The first time she thought Danny had done it and locked him in the garage with Cuddles all afternoon. Danny stood there for hours, backed up against the garage door, rigid with fear and fury, not daring to take his eyes off the brute.

But when Dad heard about the punishment, he

shouted at Aunt Mildred and said it couldn't possibly have been Danny because they'd been together the whole time. "You're a wicked and vindictive witch to throw your own clothes on the floor and try to blame it on someone else," he added, and the look on his face showed he saw her in a totally different light from before, as if a mist was finally clearing.

No matter how many times Aunt Mildred hung the clothes up, they hurled themselves right onto the floor again. It was only when Danny's dad was in the room that the clothes behaved.

"Look, I'll show you," she said to her husband, and put a dress on its hanger and into the closet. The garment just stayed there, as limp and lifeless as it should be, making her look like a liar and a lunatic.

The moment Danny's dad stepped out of the room, the dress flung itself to the floor again.

This went on for four days. Then, after twisting his ankle on a high-heeled shoe that was cunningly hidden beneath a pile of blouses, Mr. Cloke announced, "I'm moving into the guest bedroom until you get your act together."

The next morning, Aunt Mildred had a wash...and got dirtier!

So she tried to shower away the dirt...and got dirtier still.

The harder she scrubbed her face, the grimier it became. The more soap she scrubbed into her body, the smellier she became.

After bathing herself for two hours, she ended up looking like she'd been sleeping in a ditch for a month.

"Good grief!" Dad roared. "You're beginning to stink like last week's garbage!"

Aunt Mildred's rank stench had a deep effect on Cuddles. Every time the hyena spotted her, it broke out into a maniacal cackle. Neighbors were complaining about the constant noise. In the end, Mr. Cloke banished Cuddles permanently to the garage, clad the walls and ceiling with special soundproofing material and forbade Aunt Mildred from visiting it.

After three days' solid scrubbing, the wretched woman realized it was only making things worse and gave up altogether. Dad, noticing that she wasn't washing any more, said, "Now you smell like a herd of goats."

"In the words of Cyril Specter, 'a ripe *stinkulescence*'," said Danny, and gave her such an inscrutable look that Aunt Mildred wondered for the first time whether he was somehow behind all her misfortunes.

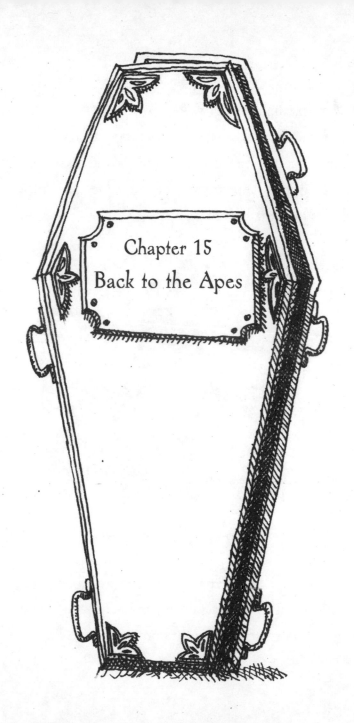

Chapter 15
Back to the Apes

BY THE FOLLOWING SATURDAY, thick shaggy purple hair was growing from Aunt Mildred's face, which she had to shave three times a day. Even her forehead began to have a sloping slant, as if she was resuming the appearance of her ape-like ancestors millions of years before.

"It's a pity you can't grow any hair back on your head," Danny's father said to her when he came into their bedroom after arriving home from work.

"I'm not going to stand for your insults!" raged Aunt Mildred. "It should be obvious to you that some sort of evil curse is upon me. And when I find out who's responsible…"

Mr. Cloke interrupted her brusquely. "When will you realize that you're the one who's responsible? You've brought this evil curse upon yourself!

"I've just had a few words with Ruth Boatswain. She's quit your store. Says you constantly ridiculed her. And worse, she told me about your lying and cruelty toward my boy. Feeding him dinners from the hyena's bowl *and* forcing him into broom closets.

"Well, all your wickedness has come back to haunt you now. I think you should leave and never darken this door again." Turning his back on her in disgust, he went back downstairs.

Aunt Mildred made a pitiful sight, standing on a mountain of her own clothes, bald and hairy, dirty and smelly.

Danny had been in his room during all this wonderful high drama. He was about to follow his dad downstairs, when he spotted something out of the corner of his eye.

He caught sight of a movement in the mirror in the master bedroom.

As Danny crept toward the room, he was in the perfect position to see what happened next.

He saw Aunt Mildred's reflection shaking with a silent rage that looked as if it was about to explode like a volcano.

Then she caught a glimpse of herself in the mirror. There was a sudden stillness in the air.

She rubbed her eyes, not believing what was reflected back at her.

Smiling out of the mirror was Cyril Specter. In a voice like the wind whipping around midnight gravestones, he said, "Action leads to consequence, Mildred, as I recently told someone else."

"No, it can't be," gasped Aunt Mildred. "Cyril Clegg, the founding member of S.L.A.Y. in this country, the finest president it ever had...until I took over, that is."

From behind the door, Danny gasped at this. Aunt Mildred knew about S.L.A.Y.!

"Yes, you are still its *stinksome* president, I hear," Cyril Specter said softly.

"Of course!" roared Aunt Mildred. "And you were one of my greatest heroes. Your books ruined half a generation of children. Why do you come back and haunt me now?"

The specter's face was stern. "A magic spell too powerful for human understanding has woven us all inextricably together. All I know is, I don't want to haunt supermarkets forever for my crimes. And your crimes are greater still. You must give up your wicked ways, Mildred. And also tell the boy what is in the old wooden boxes in the garage, where Cuddles the hyena sleeps. Do these things, and there may be hope for you yet."

There was a mad gleam in Aunt Mildred's eye. "No. Without me those weak-minded, penniless fools at S.L.A.Y. will lose sight of our great purpose and just become mere miserable librarians and schoolteachers again. We can rule the world! Crush imagination and joy in every child, now there is my great work."

"So be it, Mildred," Cyril Specter sighed.

Pointing at her he said, "Mildred Cloke, you are no more than a sickly sack of rotten meat." At these words, a speck appeared within the mirror, behind Cyril Specter.

Silently the speck loomed larger and larger. A molten ball of fury, all gnashing fangs and growling snarls, the thing was soon poised to spring from the mirror.

Aunt Mildred's mouth was working, but no sound came out.

"Cuddles," Cyril Specter called out cheerfully, "it's time for your..."

The words "sickly sack of rotten meat" were left unsaid for long moments, but Aunt Mildred understood. By the time they were spoken, the real-life, twenty-first-century wicked stepmother, the president of S.L.A.Y., had thrown her troublesome clothes, her underwear, shoes and Mr. Cloke's best razor into a suitcase, sprinted downstairs, along the patio and toward her car.

Cuddles laughed maniacally.

Then sprang from the mirror and was down the stairs in two bounds.

Aunt Mildred fumbled with her car keys. The hyena was almost upon her.

She screamed.

Cuddles pounced.

She fell into the car, backed down the driveway and

roared away up the road, the hyena in close pursuit.

Danny watched it all from the bedroom window.

Cyril Specter disappeared just before Danny's dad entered the room.

Aunt Mildred's and Cuddles' unholy stink filled the room and Mr. Cloke opened all the windows. "I don't think we'll be seeing her again," he said, and the reek that was all that remained of them slowly wafted away.

Danny watched as his dad shook his head for a moment, as if awakening from an enchanted sleep, then little wrinkles of a smile formed in the corners of his mouth.

But Danny, who never in his wildest dreams imagined that Cyril Specter could have done as spectacular a job as this, remained rooted to the spot and trembling slightly; his mouth hanging open in sheer awe of the magic that he had witnessed.

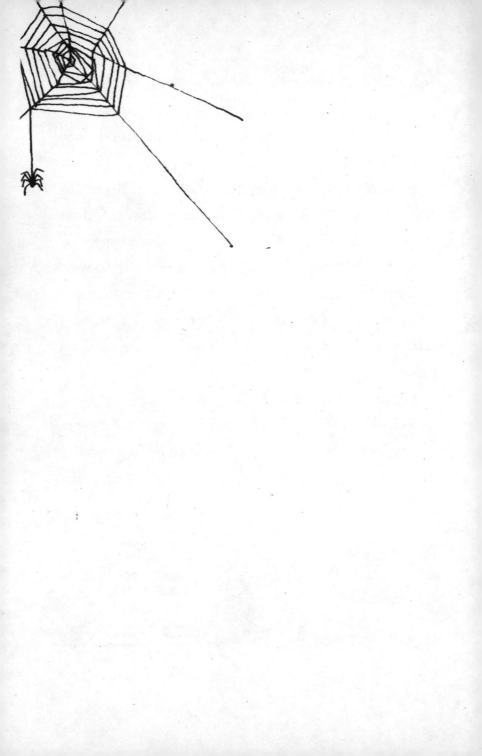

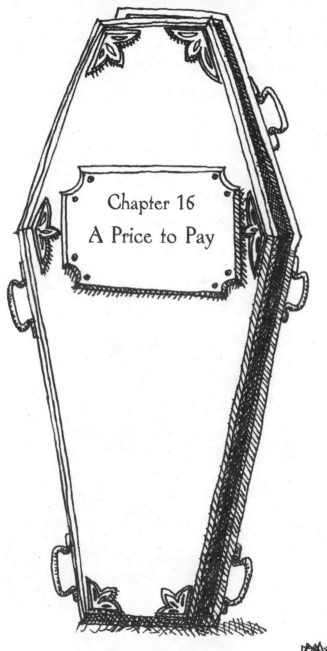

Chapter 16
A Price to Pay

LATER THAT DAY, Danny discovered that in the old wooden boxes in the garage, where Cuddles had slept, a fantastic treasure waited. Piles and piles of letters and postcards, and boxes filled with coins, bracelets, badges and photographs. He wept as he saw all the packages bore the postmark "Venezuela".

His mother had sent all this; a letter every week for the whole time she'd been gone.

There were photographs of impossibly beautiful jungles, and animals with wonderful names like

coatimundi and armadillo and capybara and kinkajou and plants called orchid-of-the-golden-crown and giant trumpet-eating dog bush.

He read the letters strictly in order. They were filled with her adventures in search of the fabulously rare bird, the Long-tailed Pink Polka-dotted Home-wrecking Cuckoo.

Night was falling as he read the last sentences of the last letter.

...and so, my son, even though this bird still eludes my camera, I've never given up hope. When I feel dark, lost and alone, I know that even a tiny light can turn into a glorious sunrise.

> *Love,*
> *Mom*

Underneath these words a little pink and white polka-dotted feather had been stuck.

And Aunt Mildred had hidden all these wonders from him.

Danny rushed inside with his treasures. Standing up from the kitchen table, Mr. Cloke took Danny in his arms. "My dear boy!" he kept saying. "My dear boy! My dear boy! Everything's going to be all right now."

In that moment, Danny loved his dad more than he'd ever loved anything before in his whole life.

They sat down to a cup of coffee and a huge plate of chocolate éclairs that Mr. Cloke had laid out lavishly on the table.

"Why didn't Aunt Mildred just throw the letters away, Dad?" Danny said after a while.

"So she could gloat over her secret, I suppose. Who knows how the evil mind works?" said Dad.

"The last letter is six weeks old," Danny said suddenly. "Do you think Mom's all right?"

"Sure," Dad said soothingly. "South America is a long way for a letter to come. She probably sends them in batches." He added with a chuckle, "Don't suppose there's many mail boxes in the middle of the jungle!"

Danny noticed his father looked pale and tired, like a victorious soldier after a long war.

"From now on everything's going to be different," Mr. Cloke promised, and tears sparkled in his eyes.

When Danny went to bed that night he must have

been the happiest boy in the world. He slept deeply, wrapped up in warm, safe dreams.

But something disturbed those dreams...

He woke suddenly, sitting right up in bed, recognizing a familiar sound; something that hinted of icy winds and cemeteries.

The house was in total darkness.

He read his alarm clock by the light of the moon. "Exactly midnight," he muttered.

Danny looked up.

Floating near the ceiling was Cyril Specter. "Greetings, Danny."

"Hi. Mr. – Mr. Specter. And thanks. Thanks for everything."

Cyril Specter chuckled. "That was a *phewsome* lesson I taught her, eh?"

"Totally *stinksome!*" said Danny, grinning.

"Absolutely," Cyril Specter said in a more businesslike tone. "Now I have to remind you that the unleashing of the wild magic of the Hero Hex was your doing and...and...I simply must demand payment. They are the terms of the spell, et cetera, et cetera."

Reaching for a piece of paper on his bedside table, Danny squinted in the darkness and read from it:

Dear Mr. Clegg,

I'm delighted to be writing you this fan letter. You are the greatest author in the entire history of the universe, and have certainly improved with age. I hope the rest of your death brings you great enjoyment.

Your greatest fan,

Danny Cloke

The boy put the letter down with a flourish, and turned to smile at the writer. "There, that's my fan letter done. Just let me know where you need it delivered to."

Cyril Specter looked grim suddenly. "It is time for you to be the Hero. You must personally deliver this letter to Under-the-Sod Cemetery before sunrise tomorrow, or I will take away that which you love most."

Bats' wings of doom and horror circled Danny now.

He felt mortally afraid suddenly, but wasn't sure why.

Cyril Specter continued, "The cemetery is only in the next village. You are to go to the holly bush in the middle and my gravestone is immediately on its right. Then, with your right forefinger, you must trace out the letters of my name where they are engraved on my headstone and when that is done, read out the fan letter, clearly and loudly, once only.

"Once this is done, the vault will vanish, and in its place will be a pit six feet deep.

"You jump down there, lie down flat with your face looking at the sky, until the earth closes over you again. You will take a turn in my grave…!"

And with that, Cyril Specter was gone.

Danny was terrified. He had until dawn. No, wait a minute, he thought, it was dawn the following day, wasn't it? It was past midnight when Cyril Specter had said, "Deliver the letter before sunrise tomorrow." If anything, it made matters worse. The longer wait made his doom stretch out even more.

"I won't do it," he said, through chattering teeth. "My punishment will be to lose my Cyril Specter books. That's all!"

He turned over in bed and tried to sleep. But the words of the spell kept echoing inside his head. "I'll lose the thing I love most. Lose the thing I love most."

"It's Dad I love most of all," he said, with a gasp of horror. "How he is now that Mildred's gone. And Mom too, her wonderful letters. If I don't complete the Hero Hex, Cyril Specter will take my parents away! Just when I've got them back. He's as bad as Aunt Mildred is!"

Danny began to think how foolish he'd been to think it was his Cyril Specter books he loved most. Of course he loved those stories. But not more than *anything* else. He had to deliver the letter. He had no choice.

Chapter 17
A Turn in
The Grave

WHEN MR. CLOKE came into Danny's room with a cup of coffee next morning, Danny was trembling and his face was a ghastly gray color.

Danny's father put the coffee down and looked at his son closely. "What is it? Are you ill? Where does it hurt?"

"I'm all right, really," Danny said weakly.

"No. You don't look at all well," said his dad and called a doctor right away.

The doctor came and examined Danny thoroughly, and when he heard what had been going on during the past few weeks, said that Danny was "overwrought" and that he should stay in bed for the rest of the day.

Danny was too tired and weak to resist. Dad brought him little snacks, talked and read to him during the day.

But when night came and the house was dark and Mr. Cloke had gone to bed, the awful suspense and terror crept across Danny again as surely as long shadows falling across a graveyard.

Every tick of his clock was a step closer to doom for him or his parents. It was one or the other. If he didn't take a turn in Cyril Specter's grave, he'd lose his mom and dad.

Danny shivered when the rusty hinges of the Under-the-Sod Cemetery gates groaned loudly, as he pushed them open.

He hurried inside, picking his way through the tall weeds and crumbling headstones, heading for the holly bush in the middle. Then he realized he'd forgotten to bring a flashlight.

It was windy with a hint of rain in the air.

Odd black shadows were formed by the moonlight on the graves. On several occasions he stopped with a cry, thinking there were deep pits opening up before his feet.

Nuzzling his face as far down into his big overcoat as he could, Danny paused to get his bearings. A cloud scudded past the moon, obscuring it momentarily.

Danny glanced up.

He froze. It wasn't a cloud.

It was an apparition!

It vanished instantly.

But Danny still stood rooted to the spot, too frightened to move.

"Come on. Come on," he muttered to himself fiercely.

"Think of Mom and Dad. I think it was only Cyril Specter, come to gloat." Stiff-legged with fear he forced himself to stagger the final steps to the holly bush.

He looked to his right and there it was.

The gravestone, with writing carved into the gray marble in fine gold filigree:

CYRIL CLEGG

Terminat hora
diem; terminat
author opus.

Nearby, the old church bell tolled eleven o'clock.

He kneeled upon the arched vault in front of the headstone. It was cold and hurt his knees. With a trembling hand, he reached out and with his finger began tracing the gold letters that formed the words CYRIL CLEGG, as he'd been instructed. He paused before the final letter, his whole body shaking.

"Get this over with," he said to himself, and thrusting his finger into the final indentation, closed his eyes and traced the G.

Then he removed the fan letter from one of the deep pockets of his overcoat, and read what he'd written in a weak, frightened little voice.

As he said the words "Danny Cloke", the words that finished the letter, he felt the ground tremble.

A tremendous roar filled the air.

The vault blinked out of existence.

Danny realized with a start that he had been kneeling on it.

He tried to scramble clear, but it was too late.

He fell screaming all the way down into the open grave.

Landing with such force that it knocked all the air from his body, Danny stared dazedly up at the sky.

Then the grass closed over him.

The blackness around him was as complete as only it could be inside a grave.

He screamed again, but this time no sound came out. He tried again. There was still no sound. He tried feeling his face.

Nothing.

He could taste nothing. Smell nothing. It was as if he didn't exist.

It was as if he was dead.

Chapter 18
A Novel Ending

DANNY LAY IN THE pitch-black trying not to panic, and failing miserably. The only sound he could hear was the blood pumping furiously around his head. He felt more alone than he ever had.

Gradually, panic was replaced by a sense of hopelessness.

Then he noticed the faint glow coming from somewhere on his right. He was surprised to find that he could turn his head, and when he did he saw a tiny speck of light in the distance.

His heart soared. "Even a tiny light can turn into a glorious sunrise," he said, remembering the words of his mother's last letter. Crawling carefully along the narrow tunnel that led away from the grave, Danny felt all his

senses returning as the light grew larger. The cold, sodden earth that soaked the knees of his pants gradually began to have a warmer and richer texture to it.

It was a carpet.

Barely a dozen yards further and he could stand upright. There was a sharp bend in the tunnel, and, without warning, Danny found himself in a dimly lit waiting room that had a ghostly quality to it. There were piles of books, an ornamental lamp covered in cobwebs, and a battered old typewriter.

In the middle of the room, sat on a battered old chair, was the body of Cyril Clegg. A spectral shape – that of Cyril Specter – floated into it.

The author was grinning broadly, and he held out his hand.

Scowling despite his obvious relief, Danny handed him the fan letter.

"The Hero Hex is broken!" bellowed Cyril Clegg/Specter. "Oh, well done, my boy! The Hero Hex is broken!" He leaped up and began capering about excitedly. "You took a turn in my grave, thereby fulfilling the bargain. The words of the Hero Hex never meant 'turn' as in 'it's my turn,' but 'turn' as in 'right-hand turn'!"

Danny was grinning now. "I must admit I thought you were monstrous when you told me what I had to do. But now I've got here, I realize how much you've done for me too."

"Absolutely right," the author said, sniffily. "If this sort of thing was too easy, you'd have every nasty little brat writing to their favorite authors about giving parents their just deserts every time they were made to do the washing or mow the lawn!"

The wall behind them began to glow, and gradually a set of gold-carpeted stairs with pictures of apples and pears on them appeared.

Cyril Clegg/Specter smiled in rapture. "Paradise!"

"What's it like?" said Danny in awe.

"I've heard it's the same as our world," said the author. "Only with nothing nasty or negative in it – ever."

A distant church bell tolled midnight.

A large hairy dog standing on its hind legs appeared at the bottom of the stairs. It smiled, and beckoned for Cyril to join him.

Cyril Clegg/Specter looked at Danny for the last time. "Terminat hora diem; terminat author opus. Which means, 'The hour ends the day; the author ends his work'. Saint Bernard waits. Goodbye, Danny. Never give up hope. It's what we've both learned, I think."

"I'll never forget you, Mr. Specter," Danny replied, and his lip wobbled as he forced himself not to cry. "You *were* the greatest writer in the entire history of the universe!"

Cyril Clegg/Specter beamed at this.

They hugged briefly, and to Danny's surprise it was flesh and not empty air that he touched. Then the author turned away.

He walked slowly across the spectral waiting room and up the stairs to a dimension where the world was a better place.

"Goodbye, Cyril Specter," Danny whispered softly. "And thanks."

Then Saint Bernard barked once at Danny...

...and Danny found himself lying on the floor next to his bed.

Under his head like a pillow was a box of frozen fish sticks.

By his side was the children's novel that Cyril Specter had conjured up from the near future when they'd first met, and which had fallen on the floor and been forgotten. Far too excited to sleep, Danny flicked on his bedside light and began reading:

Chapter 1

Dear Deceased

ATTENTION: *Cyril Clegg*
Plot 9,345
Under-the-Sod Cemetery
Upon-the-Sod
Wessex
WX1 1SOD

First day of Eternity

Dear Deceased,

The fact that you can read this letter means you are dead. I honestly hope you make a better job of death than you did of life. According to the S.A.I.N.T.s (governors of the Soul And Internal Naughtiness Tribunal), you were the most boring children's writer ever. There's more action and excitement to be found in a soggy cabbage leaf than in your stories.

Danny looked up with a sigh. As much as he wanted to read it now, it was the last book Cyril Specter would ever write and he wanted to savor it. He would read it in the morning when he was less tired.

As he placed it on his bedside table, the novel fell gently closed, revealing that the title was:

A note from the author:
Any contact with me spells death.